Friska my Friend

PATRICIA ST JOHN

Illustrated by Toni Goffe

SCRIPTURE UNION

130 CITY ROAD LONDON EC1V 2NJ

In the same series by this author:
THE OTHER KITTEN

© Patricia M. St. John 1985

First published 1985
Reprinted 1988, 1990
This edition first published 1994

ISBN 0 86201 876 5

British Library Cataloguing-in-Publication Data.
A catalogue record for this book is available from the
British Library.

Phototypeset by Intype, London
Printed and bound in Great Britain by
Cox & Wyman Ltd, Reading

Friska my Friend

Chapter one

Half past three, and on that warm, sunny afternoon in early summer, the children were glad to get out of school. They ran across the playground, pushing and jostling out through the gate. Some jumped into waiting cars but most of them turned down the road that led to the village. Colin went with them, but where the road divided he stopped and his friend Bill stopped too.

'Here,' said Bill, fishing in his satchel, 'I've got something for her. My mum said I could have the leftovers.' And he pushed a greasy paper bag into Colin's hand.

'Thanks,' said Colin. 'Coming to see her?'

Bill shook his head.

'Not now; we're going down to Gran's to tea and Mum said I was to come straight home. Maybe I'll come tomorrow. But, Col, my dad said we've got to do something or tell someone. We can't just keep on giving her things. What'll happen when we go to camp?'

Colin stuffed the greasy bag into his satchel with his school books and nodded. 'I'll tell my dad tonight,' he said. 'He'll know what to do. I wish ... oh, I do wish ...'

'Whatcher wish?'

'That I could have her,' said Colin. 'I just wish that she was mine. I'd soon fatten her up.'

Bill nodded. 'I might bring a sausage from Gran's,' he said comfortingly. 'She always

6

has 'em! Bye, Col, see you.' He ran off down the road, and Colin crossed to the lane that led up the hillside toward his home. He was quite glad to be alone because he had a lot to think about. It was a beautiful day and late bluebells and buttercups grew along the hedge. The sun shone warm on his face and from somewhere in the oakwood a cuckoo called. After a time, he turned off the lane and climbed a little track that led to the common beyond. On the edge of the common was a cottage surrounded by a garden.

The garden gate was broken and the paint was cracked. Colin rested his chin on it and looked round. The garden was choked with weeds and the grass had grown as high as his knees. The windows of the cottage were dirty and tight shut. Colin gave a soft whistle.

Nothing happened.

Colin whistled quite loudly with his eye on the window.

There was a sudden rush, and a black dog, half Labrador and half terrier, came streaking round the side of the house barking excitedly. She put her paws on the bottom bars of the gate and pushed her nose through the gap, while her whole thin body quivered with excitement. Colin pulled two greasy bags out of his satchel and fed the dog with half a pasty, some broken bread and biscuits and a cold potato. He stuck his hand through the bars and stroked the

8

thin flanks. He could count every rib. The dog nosed his face, licked his cheeks and whined with pleasure.

'Don't go,' she seemed to be saying. 'Please don't go. I need you so much.'

Colin stayed quite a long time, stroking and patting the dog and talking to her softly because she seemed to understand. 'I'm going to talk to my Dad about you,' said Colin. 'I'm going to do something. I wish you were mine, I'd soon fatten you up and you'd be the best dog in the village. But I don't suppose Dad would let me; we've got Growler already on the farm.'

He left at last, turning back and waving at the twitching black nose poked through the bars, until the track turned into the wood and he could no longer hear the short, sharp litle barks. He felt very unhappy even though he had promised to go back tomorrow. He did not yet know who lived in that cottage, but he did know that someone was starving that dog. He hurried up the lane and into the farmyard at the top of the hill; he was home.

He liked living at the top of the hill. If you looked behind you, you could see the north end of the hills rising steeply behind his school. On the other side the meadows sloped gently to the woods and hop fields and blossoming orchards of Worcestershire.

It was like being on top of the world, thought Colin, as he trotted across the yard. He went straight to the milking shed because he was quite late and Dad would be busy with the cows. He pushed past the orderly herd who stood waiting their turn outside, and went in.

His father, in his white coat, was fastening the nozzle on the udders of the cows. The electric syphon was whining and the milk was sloshing in the tank. The cows mooed contentedly; it was quite noisy.

'Dad,' shouted Colin, standing on tiptoe, 'there's a dog and she's very thin . . .'

'What's that?' asked Dad stooping down. 'The dog's all right; I've just fed him. Run in and tell Mum I'll be along in about half an hour.'

Colin sighed; it was no good trying to talk to Dad during the milking. Perhaps Mum would help him. He ran over to the house and found Mum putting a big potato pie in the oven. His sister, Joy, had just come in from her school.

'Mum,' said Colin, 'there's a poor dog and she's very, very thin. She might be starving.'

'Then we'd best call the RSPCA. Who does she belong to, Colin?'

'I don't know; it's a cottage and it looks all shut up. What's the RSP something?'

'It's a society that cares for animals that have been badly treated. If she's starving, they'll come and take her. Go and change, Colin, and then you can collect the eggs.'

About half an hour later they all sat down to their tea and Colin started again. 'Dad, there's a dog, and she's very thin, almost starving. How do I get the RS something?'

'Well, you'd best find out who she belongs to first. Where did you see her?'

'Bill and I went up the common to look for nests last week. There's a cottage at the edge of the common and it's all untidy and shut up and the dog's ever so thin.'

His father looked interested. 'That'll be old Charlie's cottage,' he said. 'He went to live there after his wife died. Strange old man, they say he is, and won't let anyone into his house, but that dog was his best friend. Old Charlie would never mistreat his dog; there must be something wrong. Why didn't you tell us before?'

'It was a sort of secret and we thought we'd feed her ourselves. Then we suddenly thought, maybe there's no one there and we'd best tell.'

'Perhaps old Charlie's ill or something,' said Mum. 'Someone ought to call in, or maybe we'd better call the police.'

'Well, he might not like that,' said Dad. 'How about Vicar? You go and tell Vicar, Colin, and ask him to call.'

Colin glanced out at the sloping shadows and the bright sky. It was still quite a long time to sunset. 'I'll go now,' he said.

14

Chapter two

Colin liked the vicar. He and Joy and Mum and Dad all went down to the Family Service on Sundays and Colin went to Boys' Club on Wednesdays. The vicar was good fun; he sometimes came to school assembly and would help with almost anything. Colin ran all the way to the main road and met Mr Dixon the vicar, at the corner. He'd been visiting poor old Mrs Brown who couldn't get out of her wheelchair.

'Hi, Colin,' said the vicar, 'where you off to?'

'To you,' said Colin, falling against him because he had been running very fast. 'Dad said I was to tell you . . . there's a dog, and she's ever so thin . . . I think she's starving . . . and the house looks all shut up. Bill and I were feeding her but we're going to camp at half term.'

'Who does this dog belong to?' asked the vicar. 'And where is he?'

'It's a she, and Dad says she belongs to ol' Charlie,' said Colin, 'and Dad says you'd best call.'

'Old Charlie?' said the vicar. 'I know him but he doesn't like being called on; never let me into the house. However, let's go and have a look.'

Colin and Mr Dixon climbed the steep lane and turned up the track. It was getting dark in the oak wood and Colin was glad he was not alone. It would soon be sunset but there were no lights in the cottage windows. They stood at the gate and whistled and the dog came rushing out whining and thrusting her nose through the gate. When the vicar pushed it open she jumped up barking. But she knew Colin and when he got hold of her she quietened down and wagged her tail.

'Feel her ribs,' said Colin, stroking her gently.

The vicar knocked on the front door; there was no answer. He went round to the back. There was a pile of bricks against a rain barrel and the dog jumped up and started drinking.

'At least she's had water,' said Mr Dixon. He knocked at the back door and tried the lock. He peered in through the windows. 'I don't think there's anyone here,' he said. 'He must have gone away. We'd better phone up the police and ask them to look into it. In the mean time . . .'

'I'll look after her,' said Colin.

'It would be best to take her home,' said Mr Dixon. 'Would your dad mind?'

'I don't think so,' said Colin.

'Well, I'm sure we can sort her out in a day or two,' said the vicar. 'She'll just be a lodger.'

'Not if I can help it,' said Colin. 'If anything's happened to ol' Charlie, I'm keeping her. She's mine.'

'Well, we'll see,' said the vicar. 'Take her home now and give her a good supper. Tell your dad I'll look after old Charlie. 'Bye, Colin, and thanks.'

'Thanks a lot,' called Colin. He kept tight
hold of the dog's collar but she didn't
struggle. She seemed glad to follow her new
master. They climbed the hill together and
when they reached the top the sun was set-
ting and the farm and the barns stood black
against a crimson sky. They reached the
house and Colin pushed open the door. The
dog walked straight into the big farm
kitchen and began poking her nose into cup-
boards and whining. The cat arched her
back, hissed and ran out into the yard.

'What on earth have you got there, Colin?' asked Mum who was ironing. 'We've got one already. Did you find old Charlie?'

'No,' said Colin. 'Mr Dixon came and he thinks the house is empty. He's going to phone the police. He told me to bring the dog home, and if ol' Charlie's gone away or something, I can keep her.'

'Oh can you?' said Mum. 'I don't know what your dad will say. However she's here now and you'd best feed her.'

She found a tin plate and Colin opened a tin of dog food and threw in a handful of dog biscuits. She trembled with excitement and wagged her tail furiously. She seemed to finish the meal in one great gulp and whined for more.

'That's enough for now,' said Mum. 'You've already fed her this afternoon. Give her some water and let her be.'

Colin sat down on the mat beside her.
She laid her head on his lap and fell asleep.
He stayed very still for a long time, fondling
her ears and stroking her until Dad came in
for a drink and a last cheese sandwich
before Colin's bedtime. Joy joined them,
grumbling about her homework, but they
mostly talked about Old Charlie and the
sleeping dog.

'Dad, if he's gone away or dead or something, can I keep her?'

'That's not fair,' said Joy. 'She ought to belong to both of us. She's littler than Growler and not nearly so fierce. I like her.'

But Colin shook his head. 'If you want another dog, you get one for yourself,' he said. 'This one's mine; just mine.'

'Bedtime, Colin,' said Mum quickly, fearing a quarrel. 'Mind you wash properly and don't you be too sure about that dog. Old Charlie may be there all the time and anyhow your Dad hasn't said you could keep her.'

Dad's mouth was full but he looked straight at Colin and Colin looked straight at Dad. Dad winked; Colin hugged him and went up to bed.

But not to sleep. Dad had to be up milking at half past four and he and Mum went to bed soon after Colin. Colin waited until he heard them come upstairs and shut their bedroom door. Joy was in her room, finishing her homework.

Colin crept downstairs on silent bare feet and the dog whined, lifted her head and pawed his knees. 'You're lonely in this strange place,' whispered Colin. 'You can come and sleep with me tonight.'

And when Mum went to wake Colin for school next morning, she nearly exploded with rage. Colin lay fast asleep with his head on the pillow and, snuggled up against him with *her* head on the pillow, lay the dog.

Chapter three

When Colin came out of school next day, the vicar was waiting for him and walked down the road with him.

'Well?' said Mr Dixon. 'What about that dog?'

'She's fine. Dad says I can keep her. What about ol' Charlie?'

'We've found out about him. The police got in and found the house empty. But there was a letter from his sister in Ledbury and they phoned her. Charlie went on the bus to spend the day with her last Saturday and was taken ill and rushed into hospital. He didn't know anything till last night, but now he's coming round and asking about the dog. I said not to worry, she was in good hands.'

'That's right. But will ol' Charlie come home?'

'I doubt it; he's had what's called a stroke and his sister thinks he'll have to stay in hospital. If he hears the dog's in a good home, I think he'll be glad to leave it at that.'

Colin stood still in the middle of the road and looked at the vicar. 'Then she's mine?' he asked.

'Seems like it,' said the vicar.

'Then you tell ol' Charlie she'll have a good home all right,' said Colin. 'I'd best get back and see how she's doing. Can I bring her to Boys' Club?'

'Er . . . I suppose so,' said the vicar rather doubtfully. 'As long as they don't all want to bring dogs. We'll see how it goes.'

'Thanks,' said Colin and set off up the lane as fast as his legs would carry him. He reached the farm very out of breath and met his dad going across to the milking.

'She's mine, Dad,' he puffed, 'mine to keep.'

'What is?'

'The dog. Ol' Charlie's in hospital and probably not coming back. I can keep her; you did say I could, didn't you, Dad?'

'Well, I suppose so; but she's to sleep in the kitchen and that's that. Understand? Your mum was real vexed finding her all wound up in the clean sheets like that.'

Colin grinned, and ran to the house. The dog came barking to meet him. He flung his arms round her neck. 'You're mine and I'm going to call you Friska,' he whispered. 'I'll let Joy take you out for a walk sometimes but you're mine, mine, mine.'

Poor Joy didn't get much of a chance because Friska would follow no one but Colin. The dog howled when Colin went to school and rushed down the lane to meet him on his return home. On Saturday he walked her far across the fields and woods and on Sunday he wanted to take her to church.

'The vicar wouldn't mind,' said Colin. 'She was ever so good at Boys' Club.'

'Don't be daft Colin,' said Mum. Friska started whining and Joy started laughing. 'You'll have her in the choir with me next,' she said.

'Now come on, come on and stop fooling,' said Dad, suddenly appearing in his Sunday suit and tie. They set off down the lane and when they reached the road the bell was tolling fast. Joy ran ahead to dress for the choir.

Everyone in the village liked the vicar and

the church was nearly full for the Family Service. Colin enjoyed the first part when the children sang or read, and the hymns, but he did not often listen to the sermon unless the vicar was telling a story. That day the vicar read a verse from the Bible twice through and then made the children say it after him:–

'The Lord says, "Do not fear, I have redeemed you. I have called you by name; you are Mine." '

And then – Colin could hardly believe it; the vicar did not actually say his name but he was talking about him.

'This week,' said Mr Dixon, 'rather a sad thing happened to old Mr Brown who lived on the edge of the common. But it would have been much sadder if it had not been for two kind, sensible boys.'

Colin blushed all over.

The vicar went on to talk about the

hungry, lonely dog and how two boys had noticed and cared (Colin turned his head and giggled at Bill). He told how he and Colin had whistled at the gate and how the dog had come rushing out and how Colin had said, 'Then she's mine now; she'll have a good home all right.'

He went on to say how the dog had come to Boys' Club but would go to no one but her own master. 'He's named her Friska,' said the vicar, 'he only has to call her name and the dog runs to him. She isn't lonely or hungry or frightened any more. She's his, and I know he'll care for her.'

Colin grinned at Dad and nudged Mum.

'And it was this,' said the vicar, 'that reminded me of this verse in the Bible.' He went on to explain that God called people to come to him, and they could either say no or answer his call, like Friska, and belong to a master who would love them and care for them; who would say to them, 'Don't be afraid, I have redeemed you; I have called you by your name. If you answer and come to me, you will be mine for ever, and safe for ever.'

There was more, but Colin was so excited that he didn't listen much to the rest of it. When it was over, Joy came running to him, looking quite proud of him. 'Fancy having a sermon all about you, Colin,' she said very loudly and the people near looked at him and laughed. The grocer said, 'Well done, lad!' and his teacher said, 'So you were the hero of the story, were you?' and

Colin went pinker than ever. But he did not linger long, for, up at the farm, his dog was waiting for him. He left Mum and Dad and Joy talking outside the church and hurried up the lane.

But as he ran, part of that verse kept going round and round in his head and he wanted to get home and say it to Friska. 'Don't be afraid; I have called you by your name. You are mine.'

Chapter four

Old Charlie never came back; he went to live in a home for old people near to his sister and Friska stayed at the farm. Colin could hardly remember the time when Friska hadn't been there, waiting for him at the bottom of the stairs in the morning, seeing him off to school, scampering down the lane to meet him on his return, all ready for a run. She was a beautiful, glossy, bright-eyed dog now and so well-behaved that no one at the farm was sorry that they had taken her in.

The summer holidays came and Colin helped with the hay, swam in the river and wandered over the countryside with Bill and Friska. At the beginning of August the boys went to camp and Joy promised to look after Friska. It was a glorious week but, when the last day came, Colin could hardly wait to get back to his dog and was nearly knocked over by her welcome.

September came and it was time to go back to school. The leaves were beginning to turn yellow and the hills were hidden by mists in the morning. The plums and apples were ripening in the orchard and one Saturday afternoon, Joy and Colin decided to go blackberrying.

'If you go down toward the hopyards they'll be best,' said Mum. 'They ripen quicker down in the valley.'

The children ran down the rutted track

that led to the distant hop fields on the
further side of the farm. To the left lay
the orchards but, on the right, the woods
came down to the track and the hedges were
heavy with blackberries. Joy and Colin
picked fast and Friska ran into the woods
to hunt for rabbits.

Suddenly they heard a furious barking and Colin, spilling half his berries, dashed in among the trees. He saw Friska dart forward, as though to attack an enormous Alsatian who was straining to reach her and growling in his deep throat. Colin seized Friska's collar just in time and was glad to see that the other dog was also firmly held, by two boys a little older than himself. They wore bright, rather ragged clothes and one carried a sack over his back. Neither they nor the dog looked very friendly and Colin felt rather scared. He made for the edge of the wood, dragging Friska behind him, still barking.

Joy had climbed the bank to see what was going on and, being as big as they were, she wasn't at all afraid. She smiled at the strange boys, asked them what they had got in their sack and offered them a biscuit each from their picnic. The boys were pleased.

The big dog had a biscuit too and stopped growling. Friska stopped barking and Colin stopped feeling afraid.

'Want to see?' said the older boy. He opened the sack and pulled out a pink-eyed, yellow-toothed ferret with dirty white fur. He pushed it toward Joy. 'Introduce you to Percy,' he said.

Joy backed. 'Ugh!' she said. 'You've been rabbiting, haven't you. How many did you catch?'

'Only two. Swagger's not much good at rabbiting; he's too big. That's a nice looking little dog you've got there. Want to sell 'im?'

'Not on your life,' said Colin quickly. It was such a terrible idea that he put his arms round Friska and held her tight.

'Where d'you live?' asked the big lad.

'Up at the farm on the hill. Where do you?'

'In a better house than yours. Want to see?'

'Yes; how far?'

'Just down by the road in the lay-by. Want to come?'

Joy and Colin looked at each other. Colin gave a little nod.

'Come on then,' said Joy, 'show us. It'll soon be sunset so we mustn't be long.'

They ran down the track until they came to the main road. A van was parked in the lay-by hitched to a trailer – a long, white caravan with scarlet curtains. A group of people sat round eating a meal. The children stopped a little way off.

'There,' said the older boy proudly. 'Good, isn't it. These are my folks. His folks live in another trailer. It'll be along soon.'

'It's lovely,' said Joy. 'I wish I lived in a house like that. Where are you going?'

'Dunno; on to the hops somewhere. Might be anywhere. Want to see inside?'

'Not now, we must go back. Mum'll tell us off if we're not home before dark. But one day, if you like, you can come and see us at the farm.'

'Thanks,' said the older boy. 'I'll do that. So long!' He smiled in a friendly way but the younger boy said nothing at all. He just stared and his bright, black eyes were fixed on Friska.

Joy and Colin hurried up the track, talking about the caravan. They thought it must be wonderful to live in a trailer, always moving on. The farm seemed quite dull. It was getting dusk and rabbits were coming out in the twilight. Friska kept rushing into the woods and the children did not wait for her. She often chased rabbits and she knew her way home.

They arrived back happy and hungry with scratched hands and scarlet lips. Mum was baking and there was a lovely smell in the kitchen. Joy and Colin settled down on the hearthrug with mugs of tea and told Mum all about their adventure and how they wished they lived in a caravan. Mum laughed and said, give her the farm any day.

'Friska's late,' said Colin suddenly. 'I wonder if she's caught a rabbit for a change. She hardly ever does. She makes too much noise.'

'Let her be,' said Mum. 'A dog wants to run and rabbit and have a bit of fun on its own. She'll come in her own time.'

Colin went to the door and stood looking out at the darkening hills. A new moon hung behind the woods and an owl hooted. He felt rather jealous of Friska having fun on her own without him. He whistled.

There was no answer; the owl hooted again. Colin stepped out into the yard and looked round. Friska must be having a very exciting time to make her stay out so long. He walked a little way to where the woods came down to the edge of the path.

'Friska,' he called. 'Good dog! Come home now. Good dog!'

But there was still no answer. The leaves rustled and some little animals stirred in the ditch; just the ordinary night sounds. No happy barking or scampering paws. Colin suddenly felt very frightened and rushed back to the house. He was glad to find his father in the kitchen.

'Dad! Mum! Joy!' he shouted. 'Friska's

not there! She never goes far. She always
comes when I call. She's gone!'

'Let's all call,' said Joy, and they all ran
outside. Up and down the path they went,
calling, calling. They went all the way back
to the place where they had picked blackberries and then all the way back home,
calling till they were hoarse. But it was no
good. Friska had completely disappeared.

'We'll have to go home now, Colin,' said Dad sadly. 'Maybe someone's stolen her. We'll get the police on to it in the morning.'

They went back into the kitchen and Dad leaned back in the armchair and took his poor, sobbing little boy into his arms. 'We'll find her, son,' he said. 'Maybe she'll come home in the night. We'll sleep with the doors open and we'll hear if she scratches.'

Joy looked up suddenly. 'Col,' she said, 'do you think that boy could have taken her? He wanted to buy her and he kept looking at her.'

Colin gave a big sniff and sat up.

'But she was with us till we were nearly home,' he said. 'I saw her chase a rabbit into the woods just below the crab apple tree.'

'He could have followed us,' said Joy. 'It was getting dark and we were hurrying. We didn't look round.'

Colin got quite excited. 'Then the police could find him,' he said. 'We know what the caravan looks like, white with red curtains. I'd know it anywhere.'

Joy shook her head. 'That one belonged to the big boy's family,' she said. 'The other one was waiting for the trailer to arrive. We didn't see it. But we'd know Friska anywhere. It ought to be easy.'

'We'll get the police on to it first thing tomorrow morning,' said Dad comfortably.

'Now how about a cup of tea, Mother, and then bed?'

Colin drank his cup of tea and went up to bed very quietly. His mother looked in later and thought he was asleep. His father only discovered their mistake next morning when he came downstairs, yawning, to the five o'clock milking and found the sofa pulled across by the door and his son curled up under a rug.

Colin was taking no risks.

Chapter five

It was a sad rainy morning and Colin came in late to breakfast, cold and wet and very miserable. He had been up early, searching the woods. He thought perhaps Friska had caught her paw in a poacher's trap, but Dad shook his head.

'We'd have heard her howling a mile away,' he said. 'I think Joy's right and she's gone with the hop pickers. I'll ring the police after breakfast.'

But the police were not very hopeful. The

hop fields were spread out all over the county and Colin hadn't seen the right trailer. They had to have a warrant to search caravans. Every caravan had one or two dogs and their owners all vowed they'd had them from birth. Stolen dogs were usually tied up inside the vans and only let out at night. Still, they'd have a look round.

'Well,' said Mum, 'we'd best get ready for church. Tidy your hair, Joy. Don't forget your tie, Dad! Colin, if you'd rather stop home, you can do so. I don't suppose the dog will come but you never know.'

Colin hesitated. He somehow felt that he would like to see the vicar, who'd been really helpful over tracking down old Charlie and who always seemed to have good ideas when things went wrong. But, on the other hand, if Friska came home, Colin certainly did not want her to come home to an empty house. He decided to stay. 'But tell the vicar why,' he said. 'He'll want to know about Friska.'

But there was no sign of Friska and Colin wandered about the yard or sat in the kitchen window and the time seemed very long indeed. He thought it must be long past dinner time but the clock in the hall told him he was wrong, although they were certainly rather late. At last he heard Joy clatter up the steps and fling open the door.

'The vicar's coming, Col,' she announced breathlessly. 'He's coming specially to see you.'

Colin ran to the window. Sure enough, Mum, Dad and the vicar were coming across the yard and the vicar had changed from his church clothes into an old jacket and Wellington boots. Colin jumped the steps and met him. 'Did they tell you?' he said. 'She's gone. Dad thinks it might be the hop pickers, but it might be a trap . . .'

'Well, if it might be a trap, let's have one more search round,' said the vicar. 'There's an hour to lunch and the sun's coming out. Look, there's a rainbow over the hills. Have you been round to old Charlie's place?'

'Have a cupper before you go,' said Mum bustling in with a tray laid with cups, creamy farm milk and home made rock buns. The teapot followed in a few minutes. They all sat round the kitchen table together and Colin felt a little more cheerful. Outside, the rainbow grew brighter and brighter and all the world looked clean and shining.

'Come on,' said the vicar, when he had drunk two cups of tea and eaten two rock cakes. 'Let's be off.'

They searched the woods right up to the ridge and down the other side. They went across to Charlie's house which was a wilderness of weeds and nettles. It was nearly dinner time and they sat down on the rough log outside the window. Colin was quite tired and very miserable again.

'Supposing Friska's caught in a trap,' he said. 'Or supposing she's gone with that boy. Perhaps she's hungry or perhaps he'll beat her. And she won't like being shut in a caravan. Friska's an outdoor dog.'

'Migrant workers are usually kind to their animals,' said the vicar. 'But, Colin, do you ever pray about things?'

Colin nodded. 'I say my prayers at night,' he said. 'I say, "Our Father which art in Heaven" and then I say, "bless Mum and Dad and Joy and me," and last night I said, "bless Friska." '

'Well, that's a good prayer. But do you ever think that there really is a Father in Heaven and you can belong to him and tell him everything and ask him to help you?'

Colin shook his head slowly. He had never really thought about it like that.

'Well, it's a good thing to know. It makes things all different. Do you remember the

54

verse you learned that Sunday when I told the story of you and your dog?'

Colin smiled. ' "Don't be afraid." I can't remember the middle bit. "I have called you by your name; you are mine." I said it to Friska when I got home.'

The vicar laughed. '*You* said it to *Friska*, but *God* says it to *you*. "Don't be afraid, Colin. I have redeemed you. I have called you by your name; you are mine." '

'What does redeem mean?' asked Colin.

'It means to buy back. It means that God loves us and wants us to belong to him. But sometimes we listen to Satan and go the wrong way and do wrong things and Satan says, "You are mine now." But Jesus came and took all those wrong things on himself when he died on the cross. He paid for them; he bought us back. Now he calls us to be his, and you can say yes or no.'

'Best say yes,' said Colin.

'Yes, much better say yes, because when you belong to God, then you have a loving Heavenly Father and you can tell him every-thing. You can tell him about Friska and ask him to help you find her. He doesn't always give us exactly what we ask for, but he loves to help and he always does the thing that is right and best.'

'It would be right and best to find Friska,' said Colin. 'Could you ask him now?'

So they prayed and asked God to look after Friska wherever she was and to bring her back. Then they left the cottage and said goodbye. Mr Dixon went down the hill and Colin went up the hill feeling much happier. If God was really so great, he must know where Friska was and he would look after her.

Chapter six

The week passed slowly and sadly. The police said they were still keeping their eyes open but, so far, they had seen nothing of a black mongrel dog. Every day Colin hurried back from school with just a tiny hope in his heart that Friska might come rushing down the lane yapping a welcome. But there was no sound except the cows, mooing as they went to the milking, or Growler's deep bark and the rattle of his chain. Growler was a big, fierce watch dog who guarded the yard but he was a comfort just then. He would put his huge paws on Colin's shoulders and lick his face and pretend to be a gentle dog. Colin would sometimes weep a few tears into his bristly coat and bring him stale buns and bread when Dad wasn't looking.

And then it was Saturday morning again and Colin woke very early. Dad was in the barn and the house was quite silent. It was a clear day with golden leaves blowing about and sprays of crimson creeper waving in the wind. Colin leaned on the sill and suddenly knew what he was going to do that day. He would have one last try. After all, Friska must be somewhere and he was nearly always allowed to do what he liked on Saturday. He thought of waking Joy and asking her to go with him but then he remembered she had to go back to school for a hockey match.

He dressed and went to the larder and found some food; two cold sausages, some pork pie, bread and butter and a slice of apple tart. He put on his strongest shoes and his anorak with a big pocket. He was ready to set off and no one must stop him. He wouldn't even tell Dad in case he tried to talk him out of it. He'd just write a note to Mum and go.

So he started off down the track, past the crab apple tree and the orchards, past the blackberry hedges till he came to the road and the lay-by where the van and its trailer had parked. It had been heading north toward Worcester and there were hop yards all the way. He would pretend he was a policeman keeping his eyes open for a black mongrel dog. It would be fun and, who knows? He might have better luck than the police.

He trotted along for hours and the warm September sun rose high in the sky. He was going along a country road between hedges fluffy with old man's beard and bright with hips and haws and bryony berries. He kept stopping to eat blackberries and did not go very fast. Behind the hedges the hop yards stretched away as far as he could see but there were no caravans; only, now and again, clusters of sheds where the pickers from Birmingham bedded down. Colin went as close to these as he dared and watched for a long time. But they were mostly locked and deserted, for the people were all out working in the fields and there were no dogs about.

He began to get very tired and sat down under a tree to eat his lunch, keeping back a sausage sandwich, in case he found Friska.

The sun was almost overhead now and he knew that he would soon come to a village, because he had sometimes driven there with his Dad, and he also knew that there was a shop. He felt very thirsty and was delighted to find that he had 30p in his anorak pocket. He could buy some Coke.

The village came in sight at last and he trailed into the shop looking hot and dusty. The shopkeeper was a kind woman and let him sit on an empty bottle case to drink his Coke. He bought a sherbert fountain and two lollipops with the change. Being nearly dinner time, the shop was almost empty and both Colin and the woman were inclined to be chatty. Colin told her all about Friska and asked her whether she knew of any caravans parked near the village.

'Well, there's three or four parked on the common through the village,' she said. 'But you be careful, my lad. What do you think you're going to do if you see your dog?'

'I'll call her by her name,' said Colin. 'She'll come to me at once.'

'And maybe there's others as will come after you at once,' said the woman. 'Don't you do any such thing! If you see your dog, you go straight home and call your dad. Your mum oughtn't to have let you come all this way alone, and you just a kid.'

'She didn't know,' said Colin. 'Are hop pickers fierce?'

'There's good and bad, much the same as

other folks. Some are really nice, some are really rough. But they won't take kindly to you walking off with what they think is their dog. Now it's one o'clock and I must shut shop and give my hubby his lunch. If you run up against any trouble, you come right back here.'

Colin set off past the cottages and oast houses and walked until he could see the vans and trailers on the common. There was quite a group of them, one behind the other. He moved a little nearer and then stopped short. The last caravan but one was long and white and had scarlet curtains and Colin knew it at once; and there was another caravan parked just beyond it and the pickers, who had come in for their lunch, were sitting round on steps and benches drinking from mugs and smoking their pipes; and right in the middle of the group lay a large Alsatian dog.

Chapter seven

There was an old stone wall at the edge of the common and Colin crouched behind it. He could not see much but he knew that he would have to wait. This was the pickers' lunch hour but later, he supposed, they would go back to the fields, leaving the big Alsatian to guard the camp. One thing, however, he had noticed; the animal was chained.

If he could creep round to the back of the last caravan without the dog seeing him, he

67

could at least whisper at the keyhole. If the boys had travelled together they had probably camped together, or perhaps Friska was in one of the nearer caravans. But if she was there, he would only have to whisper. She would know his voice at once. He wasn't sure what he would do after that. He would have to wait and see.

He waited for a long time and he felt very small and alone. Big clouds massed up, hiding the sun. Now and again he stood up and peered round the wall. The men had gone back, one by one, to the fields, and at last only one old woman remained, nursing a baby; and the big Alsatian dog.

And now his moment had come; he felt very frightened. If only he hadn't come alone; if only Dad or the vicar or even Joy were with him. He remembered that Sunday morning when he and the vicar had searched the woods and sat on the bench outside old Charlie's cottage. It had been a shining morning and earlier on there had been a great rainbow. He stood still, remembering what they had talked about. 'Don't be afraid . . . then the word that meant to buy back . . . I have called you by your name; you are mine.'

He tried to remember what Mr Dixon had said about it . . . the Father in Heaven calling us to be his children . . . we could say yes or no ... then we were his and we need never feel lonely or afraid. He would always be there loving us, helping us.

'My name's Colin,' he whispered, 'and I'm saying yes. I want to be yours. Please help me now and don't let me be so frightened.'

It was very quiet; the sun shone out suddenly from behind a grey cloud. Up in a mountain ash tree, scarlet against the orange berries, a robin sang and sang. The sun made everything look bright and the robin's song was clear and brave and happy. 'Perhaps that's God answering me,' thought Colin. 'I'll go ahead.'

He tiptoed across the common, away from the camp, until he was hidden out of sight behind the vans and trailers at the far end. Then he turned round and began tiptoeing toward them. The old woman and the dog were hidden by the last two caravans. They could not see Colin and he could not see them.

When he reached the shelter of the last caravan he crouched down and waited again for a long time, listening with his ear against the wall. Once or twice he thought he heard a scuffling movement inside. If Friska was there, he was surprised that she could not hear the loud beating of his heart.

Then he took a deep breath and did it. Creeping round the corner of the caravan, he stood on tiptoe against the steps and put his mouth to the crack below the door.

'Friska,' he called, as loudly as he dared, 'Friska, good dog, it's me, Colin. . . .'

He got no further; it sounded as though

something had suddenly exploded inside the caravan. There was a mad rush of paws, a frantic barking, a sound of furniture being knocked over, the hurtling of a body against the door. And, at the same time, the big Alsatian began barking too, straining at his lead, and the old woman came hobbling across the grass, calling out. A man appeared in the gap that led to the hop-yards, shouting, and Colin doubled up and ran as he had never run before, dodging from caravan to caravan, streaking across the common and back to the wall. But if they ran after him, they would find him behind the wall; he must go further. Doubling up again he ran uphill to where a beech tree grew with spreading roots and low boughs. It seemed made for him. He jumped, scrambled and started climbing, hand over hand, high up into the shelter of the thinner branches where no Alsatian could reach him. He snuggled against the trunk until he got his breath back, and then peeped out through the veil of golden leaves.

Everything was spread out below him; he could see the yellow bracken on the common and the hop poles stretching away toward the sky. Just below him was the cluster of vans and trailers and blue smoke rising from a bonfire and people moving about. Behind him he could see the roofs and chimneys of the village and the white road winding home. Everything was quiet again, and there was no sign of the big Alsatian. He breathed a great sigh of relief, rested his cheek against the smooth bark and closed his eyes. He felt very safe and very happy. Friska was there, in the last caravan, and Dad or the police would find her.

But when he opened his eyes, he noticed something else. The shadows were growing long and the sun was beginning to sink toward his home hills. The days were getting shorter; he had been out a very long time and he had better get moving. He shinned down the tree but he did not dare appear on the road. He crept along behind brambles and gorse bushes until the village was well in sight. Then he ran to the shop.

The lady at the counter looked up in

surprise as the little boy with scratched hands and dirty face walked in. There were several people in the shop and Colin sat down on the wooden case and waited his turn. At last she was free, and turned to him.

'Well,' she asked, 'what happened?'

Colin looked up with a big grin. 'Found her!' he said. 'At least, I know where she is.'

'Good for you. What are you going to do now?'

'Fetch my dad; could I phone him?'

'Sure; know his number?'

Colin nodded. Mum answered the phone and when she heard his voice she sounded very cross indeed and almost crying.

'Where *are* you, Colin?' she cried. 'Your dad's been searching the county for you. He's been asking at all the camps and nobody had seen you. He's just about to call the police. How could you do such a thing?'

Colin was quite surprised. 'But I told you, Mum,' he said, 'I was going to look for Friska; and, Mum, I've found her!'

'Found her?'

'Yes, but I haven't got her yet. I'm in the village shop at Leigh. Tell Dad to come at once; it's very important.'

'I told you, he was out looking for you, but he keeps phoning the house in case you turn up. Just stop where you are, Colin, and your dad'll come.'

So Colin stopped and the lady gave him crisps and pop and a stale sugar bun, even though he hadn't any money left; and he sat watching through the window and talking about Friska when there were no customers, until just before closing time, the old farm van rattled up and Dad burst into the shop.

'Where's the lad?' he asked breathlessly, looking round. Then he saw Colin sitting on the box.

'Don't you ever do a thing like that again, Colin,' said Dad quite angrily. 'Scared the life out of your Mum, you did. Now what's all this about the dog? Mum said you'd found her.'

Colin nodded. He wasn't at all frightened. He could see from Dad's face that he was really rather proud of him.

'She's in the last caravan on the common,' he said. 'You've got to come and get her with me but you'll have to be careful of the big Alsatian.'

He got up and thanked the lady very politely and promised to bring Friska to visit her another day. Then he slipped his hand into his father's.

'Come on, Dad,' he said. 'Friska will think I've gone away and forgotten her.'

Chapter eight

They got into the van and drove straight to the camp. Dad parked on the common and he and Colin walked toward the caravans. The light was beginning to fade and the hop pickers were coming from the yards. Iron pots bubbled over primuses and bonfires and the delicious smell of rabbit or pheasant stew hung over the air. A large strong man was working on the last van and his arms were covered with grease and motor oil; but

Dad was large and strong too and he went up to him.

'Evening, mate,' he said pleasantly. 'There seems to have been a bit of a mix-up. I believe you've got my lad's dog in the trailer. Can we have a look? It's a black mongrel bitch.'

The man looked Dad full in the face. 'You see our dog,' he said, pointing to the large Alsatian. 'He's he only one we've got; and if I let him off the chain you'd best run for it. Fierce as a wolf, he is. Eat your lad up in two mouthfuls if I told him to.'

They stood facing each other. Colin, still holding his dad's hand, felt a little push and he understood. He darted to the steps and called at the top of his voice. 'Friska!' he yelled, 'It's Colin. Good dog, Friska, good dog.'

Once again there was a sudden explosion and the caravan seemed to rock. Friska was

hurling herself against the door over and over again, barking and howling madly, scratching with all her might. The Alsatian also strained at its lead and barked furiously and a crowd of pickers came running up from round the bonfires. A woman's shrill voice cried, 'Let the beast out, can't you, before she smashes all the china.'

A boy ran forward and opened the door and Friska sprang out with a force that made the crowd fall backwards. 'Friska!'

shouted Colin again and she turned and leaped on him, knocking him down and they rolled on the grass together, laughing and barking. Then Colin got up and Friska stood on her hind legs, put her paws on her master's shoulders, licked his face and wagged her tail.

Another boy ran forward. 'Rover,' he called loudly. 'Rover, come here.'

Colin glanced at him. It was beginning to get dark, but Colin thought that he recognised him. Friska took not the slightest notice. Then she turned and growled at the man who had been looking on in silence. He suddenly chuckled.

'Rover,' he said. 'Rover indeed! You wait till I get my hands on you, son.'

The farmer stepped forward. 'Look, mate,' he said. 'We don't want the police in on this; there's another fortnight of picking and you won't want to shift yet. My lad's

been breaking his heart over that dog this
week past. Maybe yours thought she was
lost, maybe not, but I'm willing to make it
good to him. Take this and let's be going
and good luck to you.'

The man held out his hand and there was
a rustle of money. 'Thanks,' he said, 'and
good luck to you and your lad.'

Dad and Colin walked back to the van

with Friska bounding beside them. They drove through the village in silence because Colin was almost too happy to speak. Then as they sped up the white country road that led home, Colin leaned over the back of the seat and said, 'Dad, did you pay to get her back?'

'Why, yes,' said Dad. 'She's a good dog and worth it.' He rumpled Colin's hair. 'Taking you all round, you're not a bad lad either.'

'But she was ours already; why should we pay for her?'

'Well, finding's keeping round here, and I didn't want a fuss, not with that crowd. Besides, she got away; but you must keep an eye on her in future, Col, specially at hopping time.'

They were silent again. Now they could see the farm on the hill ahead of them, black against the last glow, and the warm light streaming from the kitchen window. Colin was longing to tell Dad all about his great day, but he was saving it up till they were all together.

'Dad,' he said suddenly, 'It's like the second part of the verse, the bit I always forget; it says, don't be afraid, I've bought you back.'

'What verse?' said Dad. Don't know what you mean ... and if your mum's vexed, Colin, remember you deserve it. You never ought to have gone off on your own like that, scaring her stiff.'

But although Mum had meant to scold, she was too pleased to see Friska and, when she heard the story, so proud of Colin that she forgot all about it. And Colin was so tired he only just managed to tell it and to swallow his favourite supper of sausages, chips and green peas before dropping asleep. He wanted to go to sleep because he wanted to wake up in the morning and find Friska in her basket by the stove.

He was up early next day and he and Friska ran out into the cool, misty morning. The grass was covered with spiders' webs and they went down across the fields and picked some mushrooms for breakfast. Colin always took Friska for a run on Sunday morning because she had to stay behind when they went to church. He specially wanted to go to church that

morning because he wanted to tell the vicar all about his great adventure, and the moment the service was over, Colin rushed up to him.

'Hey, Mr Dixon,' he said, seizing his sleeve, 'you know Friska who was lost, well, I went and found her. I went all by myself all the way to Leigh and I saw the caravans and . . .'

'Just a moment,' said the vicar. 'This is too good to hurry. I'll go and shake hands with the people and you ask your mum if you can come over to the vicarage with me. My wife will fix some elevenses and you can tell me all about it.'

So Joy promised to tell Friska that Colin wouldn't be long and, about twenty minutes later, Colin and the vicar sat down to a tray of hot cocoa and ginger biscuits in the vicarage sitting room and the vicar's wife and baby came in to listen too. And when Colin had finished his exciting story, he said, 'And you know, Vicar, it was like the second bit of that verse, the bit I forget; Dad bought him back, and when I was sitting behind the wall I was ever so frightened and I said yes.'

The vicar blinked. 'I don't quite understand,' he said.

'Well, you said that when we feel frightened, God calls us by our name and we can say yes or no, and I said yes, and it was like as though God said, "You are mine." And then I wasn't so frightened any more. And Friska wasn't frightened when I called her by her name; she came bounding out and then she was mine again, but Dad had to pay for her like you said.'

'Yes,' said the vicar gently, 'you've remembered very well. "Don't be afraid; I have redeemed you," which means, I have

bought you back. And you had to be bought back too, Colin, before you could belong to God. Just like Friska got into the wrong hands, so we follow Satan. We tell lies and are selfish and lose our tempers and Satan says, "You are mine," and you can never belong to God or go into his home. After all, if lies and quarrelling went into heaven, it wouldn't be heaven any longer, would it?'

Colin looked thoughtful. He had often quarrelled and sometimes told lies.

'So Jesus came. He died on the cross and was punished instead of us for the wrong things we had done. He paid for them instead of us so now we can be forgiven and belong to God again. That is what redeemed means. That's why we love him so much; because he loved us enough to suffer so much.'

Colin listened and nodded his head. He

had to get back to Friska but he understood what that verse meant now. "Don't be afraid; I have redeemed you. I have called you by your name; you are mine." God said it to him and he could say it to Friska. He thought about it as he walked up the lane, scuffling through the golden leaves that had already started to fall, and he felt very happy. Friska would always love him for walking all that way and braving the big

Alsatian and creeping up to the caravan and calling her by her name, but Jesus had done far more. He had died on the cross and suffered a lot of pain to redeem Colin.

'I love him too,' thought Colin. 'I'm glad I said yes; I'm glad I belong to God.' There was a wild barking and Friska came hurtling down the lane to meet him. 'And I am so very, very glad that Friska is home again.'

If you have enjoyed this story, here are some other books in the **Read by Myself** *series for you to read:*

The Other Kitten
Patricia St John
Illustrated by Gunvor Edwards
Mark and Carol go to stay with Gran at the seaside and enjoy building sandcastles on the beach. Then they discover that a friend of Gran's is giving away kittens but they quarrel over which kitten to choose. Carol runs away and gives Gran and Mark a fright. What can have happened to her? Carol has to be rescued by the lifeboat and she and Mark have time to think about the kittens. Each of them plans a nice surprise for the other.

Amy T and Grandma B
Eileen Taylor
Illustrated by Jacqui Thomas
Amy T loves spending Saturdays with Grandma B. And when Matthew's family move in next door to Grandma, she makes a new friend. Amy likes animals, especially Grandma B's cat Purrpuss. When it goes missing, Amy is the one who finds it because she can hear very well, although she cannot see.

Amy and Matthew enjoy playing in a ball pool, going to the carnival and on a day trip to the seaside.

Kangaroo Daniel and the Canal Holiday
Dilys Gower
Illustrated by Michael Charlton
Ashley is excited about going on a narrow-boat holiday on the canals. Then his parents

invite Daniel to join them and Ashley feels annoyed. He calls him 'Kangaroo' Daniel because he bounces about, causing disasters wherever he goes.

But Ashley and Daniel love the boat and enjoy helping with the locks on the canal. In the end it is Daniel who helps Ashley by rescuing him when he is trapped on the deserted boat.